AD LUMEN PRESS

American River College

Tiny Giants
101 STORIES UNDER 101 WORDS

Jason Sinclair Long

Ad Lumen Press | Sacramento | 2014

The following stories have been previously published:
"Where'd the Cheese Go?," "Balancing Racks,"
and "1976," *Fast Forward: The Mix Tape* (Fast Forward Press);
"Balancing Racks," "Gam Chammleman Takes Back His Time"
and "Weird Feet," *Burning the Little Candle* (Ad Lumen Press)

Excerpt from *Blind Willow, Sleeping Woman* by Haruki Murakami and translated by Philip Gabriel and Jay Rubin, copyright © 2006 by Haruki Murakami. Used by permission of Alfred A. Knopf, an imprint of the Knopf Doubleday Publishing Group, a division of Random House LLC. All rights reserved.

Cover image by Paul Williamson, tilt-shift effect by Ash Davies (www.photoguides.net). Used by permission.

For information address: Ad Lumen Press
American River College | 4700 College Oak Drive, Sacramento, CA 95841
www.adlumenpress.com
Part of the Los Rios Community College District

Library of Congress Cataloging-in-Publication Data

Long, Jason Sinclair, 1972-
   [Short stories. Selections]
   Tiny giants : 101 stories under 101 words / by Jason Sinclair Long. — First U.S. edition.
      pages cm
   ISBN 978-0-9911895-0-2 (pbk.) — ISBN 978-0-9911895-1-9 (Kindle)
   I. Title.
   PS3612.O4965A6 2014
   813'.6 — dc23

                              2013049293

First U.S. Edition 2014

For the grandmas, Marva & Ruth,
for always inspiring me in their tiny, giant ways.

TINY
GIANTS

My short stories are like soft shadows I've set out
in the world, faint footprints I've left behind.
— HARUKI MURAKAMI

Therefore, since brevity is the soul of wit,
And tediousness the limbs and outward flourishes,
I will be brief.
— WILLIAM SHAKESPEARE

PART ONE:
TO TASTE EXPERIENCE

PART TWO:
IT GOES ON

PART THREE: AMERICAN DREAMERS

PART FOUR:
TIME TAKES IT ALL

PART ONE:
TO TASTE EXPERIENCE

A VERY LOFTY ADVENTURE

Sam opened the book and unwittingly released a tiny blue dragon. It tore from the pages and flew into the night.

Sam followed.

WEIRD FEET

"Why would you say that?" Julie asked.

Matt stared back, shrugged.

"That's it? You say *that*, then just shrug?"

"I…," he trailed off, shrugging again.

She packed and left, slamming the door and marking the end of what they might have built together.

He ate crackers and peanut butter, certain that he was the normal one, even saying out loud, "Maybe next time."

HOT PEPPERS

At thirteen, Kirsten imagined love was like getting pushed off a cliff. You knew it might happen (you were standing near the edge after all), but when it did, you still lost your breath.

At nineteen, it felt more like eating a mouthful of hot peppers. You chose whether to eat, and once you did, only the strongest kept chewing.

At thirty-seven, love was a boxing match. Still, every so often, she stood in her garden, munching jalapeños, hoping for a precipice.

STASIS

Leaving the bundled infant on the doorstep, Trina thought, I can't believe I'm doing something so cliché. Then: I can't believe I just thought that.

She rang the bell and ran into shadow, watching from a short distance as the strangers looked left, right, left again—as if waiting for a train—and finally scooped up the child.

Trina stood alone like that for hours, waiting for something to make her move, one way or another.

THE NEIGHBOR

Watching rain run in rivulets down the outside of the window, Edward stood next to Lacey, his wife of eleven years. Her focus was beyond the window, through the rain, on Matilda.

"It's sad," Lacey said.

"Yeah?"

Matilda packed one last box into her gray Ford, then climbed behind the wheel.

"Moving's weird," Lacey said. "We'll never see her again."

She waved feebly as the old woman drove away.

"We're okay," Lacey said. "Right?"

It took Edward some time to respond and when he finally did, Lacey was in another room so she wasn't sure he'd said anything at all.

LINGUISTIC ACCOMMODATION

"Why the faux British accent?" Sasha asked.

"Have I got one?" Darren responded, half-smiling.

"Uh, yeah."

"Hadn't noticed. Must've rubbed off this past year."

Sasha handed him tea.

Darren: "Cheers."

"Welcome home, weirdo."

FATHER'S DAY

They were on the road before dawn, in the water by sunup. Within an hour they had each caught their limit.

"Must've stocked the lake."

"Seriously."

They killed the trolling motor, bobbed in the water.

"What now?"

They were drunk by nine.

DOWNHILL

Lela was a vegan and a trainer of seeing-eye dogs.

Theo fancied himself the best Ethel Merman imper-
sonator in the West.

How they met is of no consequence. Why they
clicked is a mystery of the ages. But click they did, like
two pieces completing a bizarre puzzle.

The first serious wrinkle appeared when one of Lela's
dogs pissed on Theo's favorite Ethel gown.

The rest is just embarrassing.

LANNIE, THE INEFFECTUAL SCARECROW

Enough!

He detached himself from his stick, wiped the bird shit from his shoulders, and headed for the nearest bar.

SALAD DAYS

The mother joined her son on the sofa, both entangled in a thin blanket.

"Fote," the boy said.

After a quick parental translation, sofa cushions were dislodged and a teetering makeshift dwelling arose.

They laughed, tickled each other, sang a fort song.

That night she lightly touched his forehead as he lay sleeping.

Through his dreams, he spoke lazily of fotes and mommy.

LAMENT

My college roommate Duncan kept a stash of mix tapes under his bed. Twenty copies, same mix, gifted to girls after sex.

He once explained the "science" involved, stringing them along in case he wanted more. He even carried copies in his backpack, just in case.

"Never know when you might get some."

Three months after my wife—my college sweetheart—died, I was cleaning out her closet when I came across a well-worn copy of Duncan's mix, nestled secretly in the bottom of a shoebox.

I listened to both sides over and over until I had every song memorized.

GETTING IT RIGHT

James met Melinda at a bar. They bought rounds, talked about their families, futures.

He was a Ph.D.; she owned a charming bookstore.

He offered to walk her home. They kissed, dodging moths under the porch-light and were entangled between sheets within minutes.

After daybreak, he brewed espresso for two and commented on the sunlight catching fire in her hair.

"So…," he said. "What do you think?"

After a thoughtful pause: "Little silly for me. Too… romantic? Too straight."

"Can we try again?"

That night, sporting black leather and denim, Rock the biker met Cherry the exotic dancer at the bar.

THE ROPE SWING

Dierdre walked to the end of the dirt road and stopped.

Beyond a seemingly impassable bramble of blackberry bushes she spotted it, right where she remembered.

Winding her way through overgrown trails, she thought how funny it was that even the smells hadn't changed over the years.

Finally, she held the threadbare rope in her hands, wondering if her old friend would still support her.

She backed up slowly, further, held her breath, and sailed into the sky.

THE END FOR SAMUEL BLACK

Setting up camp on a high ridge, he surveyed the valley.

He cooked, ate a can of beans, cleaned his rifle, watched the stars on their impossibly slow journey.

Morning brought a hard frost to the earth. When a jackrabbit appeared, he shot and cooked it. It tasted like being alone.

Whether it was destiny, fate, or shit luck, this was where his adventuring had taken him.

This would be his forever.

He waited.

HOUSEMATES
(ALL IN THE TIMING)

"Power's out again."

"Terrific."

"Third time this month."

"I know."

"Board game?"

"Sure."

 Later:

"Nice win."

"Thanks."

"Candlelight's mesmerizing."

"Yeah. I guess it is."

"You know, I've always kind of felt like we—"

"Nice! Power's back."

"Oh, yeah. Wow. Cool."

"What were you saying?"

"Me? Nothing. Never mind."

THE THREE-HOLE PUNCH

First you give your entire adult life to a company that pretends to care.

Next you're packing your memories into a printer box.

Other people, the ones who were spared, don't look at you on your walk of shame.

Their eyes find suddenly fascinating things inside their cubicles.

Finally you take a breath and just go for it, snatching something—anything—in a blind fury.

You're not sure what it is, but you've shown them all. You've stuck it to the man!

THE WIDOWER AND THE GRADUATE

Abe, bewhiskered and venerable, placed a hand on Tess's shoulder, alternating between a pat and a squeeze.

Tess, eyes glassy with emotion, pulled the old man in for a hug.

"I'll see you real soon, Grandpa."

He broke the embrace, held her at arm's length.

"You be careful over there."

As they pulled out of the gas station in opposite directions, they shared a single thought.

It was a little about hope and a little about fear.

OUT TO SEA

Fishing had never come easy to Douglas, although fighting was second nature. He had a hard time hooking a salmon three feet away, but he'd kick someone's ass out of reflex.

His first day on a deep-sea boat would prove to be his last.

It was a sight to behold: Douglas leaping overboard to battle an errant marlin, smiling as he was pulled under and into the great blue brine.

INSIDE

This isn't your typical coming-of-age story. I mean, yeah, I came of age. We all do.

But instead of heartbreak at puberty, I killed two guys in an alley when I was fourteen. How's that for losing your innocence?

It wasn't self-defense, not really. More like protection, a little retaliation.

I'm paying for it; I'll always be paying for it. Free tattoos though, and I'm learning to cook in here.

So I've got that going for me.

ONE FOR THE STORYBOOKS

Despite her black-haired and black-eyed and black-lipped 80s-era Gothic veneer, and regardless of her hammering a heart-shaped pattern of nails into his dorm room door on Valentine's Day, and notwithstanding the mix tapes comprised entirely of her breathing heavily between Bauhaus songs, somehow Preston—straight-laced, upper-class, Connecticut-bred Preston—fell for Bethany, and, even better, they lived long and happy lives together.

THE GOOD SON

"We'll do it tomorrow," the father sighed.

"You said that yesterday," the son replied.

"You'll understand someday," said the mother. "These things happen."

That night as he lay drifting into the cradle of sleep, the son vowed to never understand it.

And he never did.

H. & S. IN REAL LIFE

Harry met Sally.

Harry got Sally.

Harry lost Sally.

Then, instead of getting Sally back (and due in no small part to his propensity for screwing up over and over), Harry never saw Sally again, because Sally found true love with a man who didn't fuck things up.

STEPHANIE AND ALEXANDRA

We found a baggie of pot hidden in Steph's dad's garage. It was rolled into a neat hot dog shape. I thought she'd be scared to, but we stole it.

We hiked out beyond her property, to the pond, where we met some boys who were torturing a broken-winged bird.

Steph's eyes kind of squinted and one side of her mouth smiled. "Trade you," she said, offering the weed.

We carried the bird home, taking turns holding it in our palms. It died an hour later in Steph's room, but it was still a good trade.

HIGH SCHOOL CASSANOVA

The first time they held hands, she swore she'd die. Every sense bubbled, popped as his fingers played around hers. Leaning her head on his shoulder, she sighed pleasantly.

"Yo, Brandon!"

As fast as it had been cast, the spell was broken. He jumped up, high-fived his pals, disappeared.

She sat the party out, alone, watching him bounce and stumble from room to room.

Later, she daydreamed of prom and traced the numbers on the back of his jersey while he vomited again and again into the kitchen sink.

IN FLEW THE *ELEGANCE*

None of them could believe what they were seeing.

Everyone knew spaceships were supposed to be enormous.

But here the tiny craft hovered, above the kitchen sink, its name inscribed inexplicably in English.

BALANCING RACKS

Victor couldn't remember the last time Stella wanted to play Scrabble period, let alone all night.

Next morning, dead even, they stared through glassy eyes and went one more.

Stella triple-worded her way to victory.

"Feeling superior?" Victor asked.

She hummed lightly, smiling in reply.

He boxed the game, shelved it, brewed Darjeeling.

She opened a window, let in the air.

"I cheated," Stella said, at last.

"I know."

"Not at Scrabble."

"I know."

They held their tea close, warming their hands against the worst of it.

PART TWO:
IT GOES ON

WARMING

As the snowman began to melt back into the earth, he realized his fate and calmly acquiesced.

EMPATHY

"It's not that I *can't* understand it—I *choose* not to."

Alisa spoke without a hint of irony.

Seth sat across the table from her, silent, incredulous.

She stabbed scrambled eggs with her fork, talked with her mouth full.

"I mean, seriously. I'm capable of seeing it through her eyes. It just doesn't *benefit* me to do so. You understand. Right?"

OUT OF GAS

Landon pulled into a station, filled the tank, waited to pay, checkout counter empty.

From inside the office behind the counter, voices.

A woman said, "By nine."

"You'll be home when I say, bitch!"

The sound of something heavy being thrown, a door slamming, tires squealing. A woman maybe twenty-one emerged from the office to ring Landon up. Her eyes were puffy, red.

Landon waited, watched her. Their eyes met.

"Where you headed?" she asked.

"Chicago."

Her eyes questioned.

Landon nodded.

She snagged a six-pack of something caffeinated and some chips, leaving the keys to the station on the counter.

RE: MISSION

Lock picked, they immediately realized their school hallway was unnerving after dark.

The emptiness, silence, chiaroscuro lighting made for an eerie scene.

"Let's do this."

They stealthily trekked to Mr. Hunter's classroom, made quick work of their mission there.

Next day, the school was abuzz about the welcome back banner: "WAY TO KICK CANCER'S ASS!"

NONPLUSSED

The last time she saw her parents, Irene left in a rage, flipping them the bird through the window of her 1968 Beetle.

She hadn't forgotten the look on her dad's face: a puzzling pastiche of regret and release and fatherly concern.

That was two years ago; much had happened since then.

Irene met Jeff, for one, and their announcement was reason for reconciliation.

The stranger answering her parents' door—informing her that the previous owners now called a Winnebago home and that, no, they hadn't left a forwarding address—could only shrug when Irene said, "Seriously?"

INTO DUST

They awoke covered in fine dust, plagued with eye-numbing headaches.

"What happened?" Taylor asked.

Stein was silent, taking in their environment, the dust covering their suits.

"We're stuck here."

"What?"

Stein held a powder-coated sleeve aloft. "This is the machine."

"Deteriorated?"

Stein laughed.

"The components," he said. "Circuitry, wiring…"

"What about them?"

"They don't exist here, in this time."

"Wait," Taylor offered. "We don't exist here either, so how—?"

He couldn't finish his thought as first his lips and then his startled eyes and then everything else disintegrated into the cosmic wind.

FLOATING

Elliott sat on the dock, his feet dipping just below the lake's surface. The cold water grounded him, providing a sensation to match the numbness.

It was a week since the accident, but felt more like one prolonged immeasurable moment, stretched forever outward.

Breathing on autopilot, Elliott felt a pulling inside, an aching tug at his core. He swiveled his head like a periscope, aiming his expressionless eyes at the stars.

He spoke her name once and slid like a broken marionette into the water.

PILGRIMAGE

She'd never been out of her hometown, let alone overseas.

Paris smelled like bread and urine.

In Amsterdam, she was mugged outside a crooked building.

And her time in Prague was little more than one long lonely hangover.

Flying home, she felt life surge in her bones.

A DOG'S LIFE

When Malcolm was a boy, he wanted so badly to be like his dog that he copied Barky's every move.

He found an obvious home when a traveling freak show snapped him up on account of his ability to lick his own asshole.

FOREVER "IT"

"Effortless."

Art class, last day.

"Insipid."

Our professor—Anish Blumenfeld, famous Hindi-Jew—looked like he'd vomit with anguish when evaluating work.

"Brave."

We pretended not to care as he waved a hand, passing judgment.

"Contrived."

One word sealed fates—people became dropouts or found instant success in SoHo galleries. His verdicts were legendary.

Anish approached my painting, eyes bulging.

I held my breath.

"It…"

Clearing his throat, he clutched his left arm with his right hand. Face draining of color, he fell to the floor.

We all stared as the ambulance pulled away, its sirens as silent as we were.

PINKY

Puzzled by what they were calling him but not one to hold grudges, Simon tried to focus on midterms.

The possibilities, however, continued to tug at his thoughts.

Did Rebekah start it? Or Sera? There was that one-night stand after the dorm party. What was her name? T-something?

He imagined calling them all together to hammer out the details, a kind of sexual Council of Nicea.

In the end, he accepted—no, embraced—his new nickname, deciding to wear it with pride.

GOOSE ATTACK!

"No way."

"I'm telling you, a whole damn flock!"

"Gaggle."

"Huh?"

"Geese in a group are a gaggle."

"Seriously?"

"Everyone knows that."

"I thought birds were a flock."

"Seagulls, yeah. Not all birds."

"Like what else?"

"A murder of crows, for one."

"Well, these geese thought they were crows then."

"They attacked you?"

"Among other things, yes."

"Wait a second. What does that mean?"

"Never mind."

IDAHO UNDERCOVER

Low clouds.

Deer.

The hectic sound of hardcore filling every room in the deserted house. Emptiness for miles.

You finish shaving your head. Eat days-old pizza. Snort lines off a shard of broken mirror while Trent and Killer plan another attack, this one on a whole family.

Tonight you'll put these two away.

If you don't fuck it up.

You hold your breath.

And wait.

SIB OUTING

For their first public outing as an official couple—
Hilary's annual costume soiree—they decided to dress
as Hansel and Gretel. Five different people said it was
awkward for lovers to come dressed as siblings.

These comments only made them play it up more:
they kissed, held hands, giggled with delight.

They were as surprised as everyone when Theo and
his sister Tillie stormed out of the party in tears.

SASSY PANTS

Everyone tells her they're hideous, but there's just something about them.

Her first day wearing them she's asked out three times and offered free swim lessons at the Y.

Before bed she folds them neatly, tucks them into a drawer, whispers sweet nothings into their pockets.

Sometime after midnight she wakes and finds them making out with one of her sweaters.

THE REVOLUTION WILL
NOT HAVE A DRESS CODE

When Xavier started wearing suits to school everyone took immediate notice.

His teachers agreed he looked more grown-up, while his fellow students found new reason to jest at another's expense.

In time, of course, everyone began to follow suit: boys perfected the art of the full Windsor; girls found tranquility in fancy dresses.

Then one day, Xavier came to school in ripped jeans and a stained Hello Kitty t-shirt.

For days, no one knew quite what to do.

THE DEATH OF HER

By the time she cleared away the cobwebs and opened herself up to the world, Sandra seemed too old to enjoy what she found: people, parties, marathons, skydiving.

If she didn't die trying, no one ever did.

FAMILY SNAPSHOT

My dad spent four years in Vietnam. His dad fought in Germany during World War II. And I'm sure a great-great-someone killed or got killed during the Civil War.

We're Norwegian, so someone way back was probably a conquering Viking.

You get the idea: the Gaarder boys have war bones.

Until me.

There's a photo taken when I was twelve that says it all.

While I *demi-plié* in the corner of the room, the others arm wrestle, pretending I'm not there.

MADE IN HELL

Celeste was a vampire of the highest order. Frank was a zombie from the wrong side of the tracks. Their parents, of course, forbade any connection between them.

They, of course, fell in love anyway and met on moonlit nights by secret rendezvous.

She never tried to turn him; he never even thought about eating her brains.

BABY STEPS

Laminated nametag in place, Lucy Callow stepped into the auditorium.

An imposing primrose and azure banner requested the pleasure of her company with its ostensible greeting: Diving Into Lake You!

Leaving the seminar before it began was the first step.

INTERVALS

In one moment in time…

A little boy named Lincoln stole his first base in a ballpark in Chicago.

Susan Diller, a 3rd grade teacher in Springville, found $300 on the sidewalk.

A speeding Corvette lost control, flipped several times, and landed on its wheels, leaving only minor injuries inside.

Duke, a German Shepherd lost for two years and presumed dead, finally found his way back home.

A twelve-year-old girl named Penny cashed in her savings for a 1969 Ludwig drum kit.

And the moment after that….

WHIRLING DERVISHES

Another argument, this one involving mom, dad, and both kids.

Shelia had become something of an expert at drawing emotional lines and hunkering down behind them. Dennis should have seen the detonation coming. Holly knew she was arguing just to argue but kept on anyway, propelled by her own racing heart. And Scotty just loved a good fight.

"This family sucks ass!"

"Your attitude sucks ass!"

Turning away, Dennis closed his eyes, pulled chin to chest, and started to spin.

The others watched, stunned, silenced. Slowly, one by one, they joined him.

They were still spinning when morning arrived.

CAMP WANANUKA

"The night air feels good."

"Totally."

They walked for a while in silence, breathed in the piney atmosphere.

By the pond, he stopped, took her hand, kissed her. Reciprocating, she wound her fingers through his hair.

"So, like, you put out, right?"

The shiner, like his own purple badge of courage, still decorated his left eye when his mom picked him up a week later.

SOLACE

Yesterday the last of my friends passed on.

I was in my alfalfa field when his horse clomped up to me, empty-backed and neighing.

Despite the law, I buried his body on my back acreage.

Tonight I'll let my oil lamp burn till morning.

1976

Johnny Woods from Philly beat the shit out of me the day he started at our school.

I vowed revenge and got it, but not how you think. All through junior year, my every attempt to take him down failed—he was always at least a step ahead. Finally, bigger forces took care of it for me.

Word spread fast: Johnny had reached into the washing machine at the wrong time. Agitator took his arm off at the shoulder.

Wish I could've just kicked his ass or something instead.

PART THREE:
AMERICAN DREAMERS

BARON VON CRACKERS, THE POST-APOCALYPTIC CLOWN

He tried everything: juggling, unicycle, slack-line. Without an audience, it just wasn't the same.

WHAT LIES AHEAD

Somewhere inside, Alice knew she was letting Fyodor lead her to very dark places.

It wasn't just the heroin. There were also other... misadventures. But even if she had someplace else to go, could she?

Alice sat at the bus stop, eyeing traffic, considering her prospects. She checked her watch, rubbed aloe on her cold sores.

The veins in her arm cried out beneath her track marks.

A thin balding man on a passing bus stared out the window at her.

He smiled.

She smiled back, her lips cracking. The blood on her tongue tasted like warm pennies and possibility.

THE FUTURE PERFECT

I'm in a neighbor's car, staring out the back window, watching the fire take everything, its impossible yellow heat reducing our entire neighborhood to ash.

Tonight we'll stay in a shelter with other lost families.

Dad will pick a fight with a plumber for no good reason; mom will play cards with housewives she's never met.

I'll meet a girl new to Woodside High; we'll share a beer she has smuggled in.

By morning, I will have had the most amazing, vivid dream.

THE FIRST TIME IS ALWAYS THE HARDEST

The night Gerald got bit, a thin white sickle hung in the sky.

So much for werewolves and full moons.

His first transformation was painful beyond belief.

He broke a rib, jammed his thumb, bit himself in the ass.

Things were considerably easier after that.

LAND, GRANT!

Above the treetops now.
Neighborhood kids yelling: "Grant!"
Floating higher.
"Grant!" mother cries.
By nightfall, he is a speck against the moon.

COMBUSTIBLE RIME

They were fire and ice: he a pyrotechnics expert, she a glacier researcher.

Hollywood brought them together and would one day tear them apart.

But in the meantime—and that's the part worth remembering—they complimented each other in a way rarely experienced. Or seen.

All future relationships would be funhouse mirror reflections of that quintessential one.

SEA CHANGE

Maggie adjusted one end of the prayer flags she had hung over the door. Then she burned incense and sipped spicy chai.

When the students began trickling in, they held nothing back.

"Whoa, smells like my crazy uncle's house."

"I hate incense!"

"Ooh, I like it."

"You would."

After the tardy bell, Maggie stood and addressed her new class.

"I'm Margaret Tillman," she started. "But please, call me Maggie."

She hadn't meant to start a revolution, but things at Jefferson Junior High would never be the same.

CUT THE SHIT

Whatever it is you're thinking, it's wrong. I ain't no softy and I ain't no pushover neither.

Hell, I almost killed a guy for calling me less than that.

Kicked him in the head.

It's just that she was sick and needed help. So I helped her.

Don't tell me you wouldn't do the same thing.

EL DIA DE LOS MUERTOS

It lasted exactly ten years.

After the haunted house debacle and the trip to the ER, they felt they owed the old man something. But pity quickly turned to friendship as they realized genuine feelings for him.

They fished, drank, argued, hugged.

Then, by way of stroke (not heart attack this time), he died.

Instead of flowers they place candied skulls on his grave.

THIS LIFE

He leaned back into the sofa and stared out the window.

In the newly constructed garden, his wife planted fledgling tomatoes.

He watched her work methodically, delicately. He thought of their son, napping upstairs, and he imagined what kind of dreams an eighteen-month-old might enjoy.

The anxiety that had crippled him for days began slowly to recede. He breathed deeply and with purpose.

Again.

SPARE A BUCK?

Canine-throated, his voice barked up from the dirt grime shadow stink of the streets.

I was broke, so all I could think was to sit with him on the curb and share a few words.

What he had to say made sense and so I stayed.

And so I stay.

And here I am.

THE LATECOMER

The ghoul crawled from his grave, setting forth on a mission of fright.

Making his way into a quaint neighborhood, he stopped outside a particularly lively house. He smiled a gruesome rotten-toothed smile as he peered through a window at scores of potential victims—they danced feverishly and laughed with opened mouths and drank brightly colored liquid from a punch bowl.

The party's host opened the front door just as he limped onto the porch.

An hour later, his cannibalistic plans dashed, the ghoul smiled sheepishly as he was awarded Best Costume.

WIDE OPEN

He opened the window despite the cold, inhaled the atmosphere.

The weather always made him think of life with her. When the sun split the clouds, he remembered that time in San Diego. Heavy rain brought thoughts of Ireland; snow, Tahoe.

This time of year—with its constant falling— brought memories of her exit.

He sat at the window for hours, watched the trees in the yard, thought about her favorite poet.

A leaf falls.

Loneliness indeed.

PRE-TEEN SPELUNKING

The three of them—Jimmy, Thaddeus, Ursula—made their way into the mouth of the cave.

Breathing deeply, as if about to go under water, they descended into the vast darkness. Even their whispers echoed down and back.

Seven minutes later, Jimmy in the lead, they found an exit.

"Well, that was lame," Thaddeus announced.

"Yeah," Ursula added.

Jimmy nailed the mood: "Told you we should have gone bowling."

AMERICAN DREAMERS

She was no Sleeping Beauty, being annoyingly energized and overly reliant on a variety of facial and hair products. And he was certainly anything but Prince Charming, his proud addiction to internet porn providing unequivocal proof of this fact.

They met in a pool hall, she with her sorority gals, he in a Jäger-induced stupor. Their first kiss chipped a tooth and bloodied a nose.

After their wedding, ad fiasco in its own right, they bought a fixer-upper in Bakersfield.

Kids, four.

Separations, five.

Livin' the dream.

THE BIRDING WORLD

The most surprising thing to Charles wasn't the sheer number of birds out there but rather the fact that *they* appeared to be watching *him*.

FALLING STARS

One thing Kalen had never understood was making wishes.

What a waste, devoting effort without any possibility of affecting change.

And here he was, in a vast desert, camping with a bunch of wishers. They sat around a crackling campfire, knees drawn up for warmth, and craned their necks, eyes skyward, waiting.

Kalen missed the entire shower, zipped in his tent and snoring before the first dozen appeared, their tails carving momentary scars across the night sky.

BUCKY CALLED DIBS

We were all totally jealous and still arguing over seconds when Bucky picked it up, all heavy and metallic.

Vic swears his tongue was pressed against his teeth ready to call it first, but then he swallowed his gum and got beat to the punch. And Danielle found the thing in the first place.

But it was Bucky who messed with the trigger and whose eyes ballooned and skin grew white after the gun went off and Danielle fell over sideways, the fresh blood on her T-shirt slowly staining Bob Marley's face a deep crimson.

ANNUAL

She sits on the deck, staring blankly out to sea. The wind blows pollen in ghostly sheets across the yard. A deer stands, chewing bits of sagebrush, sizing her up.

Her focus narrows on an incoming wave, the rolling movement of a dancing apparition. She stares, unblinking, until the salt in her eyes joins with that of the ocean air.

This: every year, for one day, to remember him.

THE INNOCENT MAN

Cornered, he lashed out, becoming the monster for which they searched.

GRIDLOCK

As worldviews grew increasingly pessimistic (drinkable water drying up), Suicide Booth lines grew longer.

Crowded masses of customers jostled their way towards certain death.

Then, overloaded, everything stopped working. And a little girl with hope for eyes started pulling people away.

UP

Leaning the ladder against the house, Ella positioned her right foot a few rungs up. She took a deep breath and climbed.

Reaching the top, she placed her hands on either side of the ladder and surveyed the surface before her.

Damp clusters of fallen oak leaves clung here and there to the rooftop.

She hoisted herself up, surveyed the workload. This had always been Scott's job, every fall, until the last.

She imagined him up here with her.

Lifting the broom, cradling it against her breast, she began to sway gently from side to side.

NEW FRONTIER

Donny wondered, What does one do to avoid succumbing to hermeticism and dying alone?

Meet the world, he decided.

For years he friended as many people as possible.

His Facebook list spiraled into the thousands. He made phone calls, wrote emails, texted incessantly, even maintained a blog about origami, yet something inside kept tugging. Then, one Tuesday night in May, he dreamed he was eaten by an octopus with cameras for eyes.

Within a week, he'd swan-songed every mode of communication, boiled the excess from his life down to a single backpack.

Eventually they all stopped wondering about him.

WEST

Walter looked up and saw clouds where only moments before he was sure there had been none. He watched one long enough to see it change shapes several times. A clock, a gun, a face, something resembling Walter's idea of hope.

Was this a sign telling him his move was the right idea? Or just clouds?

Maybe a little bit of both.

WHERE'D THE CHEESE GO?

None of us can remember why we started calling Grandpa "The Cheese" in the first place.

But that was the last thing on our minds the night he disappeared.

Hours of panic, phone calls to friends, combing the neighborhood…nothing.

It was after midnight when he came down from the attic burdened with newspaper clippings and photos of the old days and cheeks streaked with tears.

PART FOUR:
TIME TAKES IT ALL

NEXT IN LINE

The fish swam excitedly toward his school.

"Look," he said, eager to show off his newness, "I've evolved!"

And he blinked.

HOME

Moving from a resort town to a nearly deserted one taxed my nine-year-old soul.

Dirt-broke and dirty, we could barely afford food.

"A new house?" I asked, when Dad surprised us one day.

"Well…new to us."

Later, we faced a ramshackle farmhouse, its faded red paint blistering before our eyes. Windows shattered by vandals, doors stolen to fuel teenage bonfires.

"This is it," Dad said. "Home."

He stood, arms spread, as if showing off an exquisite piece of art.

I looked at Mom. She smiled, just a little, and I swear I saw gears starting to turn behind her eyes.

THE (DOUBLE) DEAL BREAKER

"I'm not compensating for anything!" Cliff squealed, his voice snagging on a momentary resurgence into puberty. "I just like big trucks."

With that, he struggled into the driver's seat of his Ford monstrosity and drove off, leaving Margaret in all her knowing on the sidewalk.

RADIANCE

The morning was unusually dim under a cotton-choked sky.

Somewhere a woman suddenly couldn't remember her own name.

Seven hundred miles away her estranged son snapped awake from deep sleep.

He was oddly compelled to speak a word he hadn't thought of in years. "Belinda," he said to an empty room.

The clouds over her home parted just so.

TURNING BACK

Like a single-purposed machine Stacy systematically destroyed all evidence of her relationship with Madison.

Photos of their Jamaican yoga retreat: deleted.

Romantic letters in Maddy's unmistakable hand: shredded.

Anniversary lingerie: repurposed into flimsy, ornamental cleaning rags.

Stacy let the trashcan lid fall closed, suffocating the last of the remnants.

She breathed deeply, her mind muddled by oxygen and remorse.

THE CHEATER

"It wasn't me!"
"Yeah, right."
Then Billy Donnell kicked my ass.
Truth is, it *was* me.
And I'd do it again.

1989

The world changed.

Forever.

The Berlin Wall came crashing down. The first gay marriage was recognized. And I made out with Chloe Canter.

Seven times.

GAM CHAMMLEMAN TAKES BACK HIS TIME

It took nearly eleven years, but he did it.

First, the teachers who had stolen so many hours with lectures and brainwashing.

Next, the bus drivers and flight attendants who had repeatedly made him wait.

Finally, the girl at the diner who never seemed to notice him without prodding.

He buried them all in the backyard and sat staring at the sky. The light from the sun soaked into his hair, which he realized had somewhere along the way turned a dazzling gray.

THE DAY DING-DONG BECAME DAVID AGAIN

Hookas, bongs, vaporizers.

Jimmy and Ding-Dong had a collection envied by most in Santa Cruz.

They had shared everything—first a dorm room and then an apartment, sleeping till noon, waking and baking—for the past five years.

Imagine Jimmy's surprise, then, when Ding-Dong announced his retirement the day after they graduated.

"Seriously?"

"Seriously."

"What about the collection?"

"It's yours."

"Bro...," was all Jimmy could muster.

"You'll see me around."

But he didn't.

FEEDING GROUND

Wayne had already tried and failed in several support groups when he realized the fifth psychiatrist in a row was going to be unable to "fix" him.

It wasn't that he necessarily got off on the sight of blood, but, because he had developed a fondness for a certain kind of aftermath, he rented an apartment near a particularly dangerous intersection and spent his nights smoking and watching the red cars. They tended to be the most reckless.

DAY AFTER DAY

"You're always walking away from me," she said.

"Huh." He shrugged, noncommittal.

In truth, he did it accidentally but enjoyed her thinking that it was on purpose.

DANCING SHOES

She awoke in a hospital bed, her legs numb weight beneath the sheets.

All memory of the accident wiped away, her tearful thoughts now focused on one question.

Falling into a fitful sleep, she came to when her father arrived for visiting hours.

Before she could ask the obvious, he withdrew two delicate items from a paper bag, placing them gingerly on the bed.

"Really?" she cried.

He nodded and wept with her, smiling all the time.

METAMORPHOSIS

Three years now I've been squatting in rich people's vacation homes, sleeping between their Egyptian cotton sheets, pissing in their glistening toilets, swimming laps in their salt-water infinity pools.

The idea of caviar used to make me sick to my stomach.

Now I can't go a day without it.

RIPPLE

Henry and Celeste sat in a café, staring into mugs of coffee and tea, respectively.

Between them, a photograph of a child half-covered a baby blue piece of paper with the image of two hands held in prayer, only one hand and a snippet of psalm visible.

"I don't think I can go home," Henry said.

Celeste said nothing, dropped her finger into steaming liquid, stirring granules of black tea about.

"Isn't that hot?"

"Incredibly."

He looked at her face, wanted to touch it, to set back time.

"We'll get through this."

She let the tea burn her finger red.

AMOUR

Romantic ninja he was not; nor was he a pirate of love.

He never broke a promise or a date.

He always *tried*.

POISON CONTROL

Cousin Billy noticed it first. He was transfixed with something in the palm of his hand.

"Look how these little sugar balls melted."

Aunt Sue looked over his shoulder as he rolled a silvery fluid toward his thumb and back again.

"I didn't use sugar balls."

Soon the whole family was involved.

"What is that?"

"Looks cartoony."

Aunt Linda suddenly leapt to her feet, gasping. "Where's the turkey thermometer?"

After the phone call, as everyone lined up to heave Grandma's delicious dinner into the single bathroom's toilet, they thought their thanks might be better saved for another time.

TROMPE L'OEIL

Rita adjusted her skirt, rolled her lips over one another, evening her lipstick.

Her tongue scoped along the surface of her teeth for loose bits of lunch. Finding none, she smiled eagerly.

He walked closer, her Adonis, her future.

Then, in one slick motion, like an illusionist performing his signature move, he withdrew a cigarette from out of nowhere, inserting it magically between his lips.

In an instant she vanished.

7TH GRADE

We were in the cafeteria, eating, laughing. For all the reasons kids do stupid things to each other—because his shoes were different, because he was skinnier, because his parents were still married—I thought it would be funny to sneak peanut butter into Jordan's Oreos.

Everyone knew he was allergic, but we didn't understand what that meant.

He ate one and then for a long time everything happened in slow motion: paramedics, funeral, school assembly, grief counseling.

Even now, decades later, I see him somewhere in my own son's blue gaze.

I swear he stares right through me sometimes.

THE CURSE

She knew the curse probably wouldn't work, but she did it anyway. Just in case. Because you never know.

He was cooking an egg when the pain hit: right knee, sudden, shooting. Then stomach; he doubled over.

She wrapped the doll in a paper napkin he'd once used at McDonald's, stowing the mummy-like thing in a small box, stashing it behind *Bulfinch's Mythology* in the public library.

He grew thin and old, surrounded by doting family: wife of fifty-two years, two sons, three daughters, eight grandchildren, one great-grandson, and the family dog, Murray.

Her death rattle filled an empty space.

WANDERLUST

He slid the window closed against the cold and half-watched the passing cars.

Unable to figure out why she'd left, he played the last several months over in his mind.

He shook his head, sighing through his nose.

A year later the postcards started landing in his mailbox: Amsterdam, Santiago, Tokyo.

He read the first few, but after that he started dropping them unread in Dumpsters around the city.

Maybe some homeless guy would give a shit.

CURTAINS

When his final hour was upon him, Parrish realized he shouldn't have built a life on lies and betrayal.

Eyes closed, he whispered prayers for forgiveness to a massive, empty room.

The thin echo of his own voice came back to him like a kaleidoscopic theme song, scoring his fevered conscience, fetching his last breath.

OUTFOXED

Wanda reclined in nothing but a peach negligée, extravagantly puffing a menthol cigarette. She exhaled delicate smoke rings, smiling at memories of the night before.

The vague shape of Tony from down the block, ostensibly hired to mow her lawn, was still molded into her satin sheets.

It had been devilishly easy for Wanda to overcome his Christian objections and seduce him, his reticence and naiveté turning to mush when confronted with the sight of her bare skin.

Opening her jewelry box to retrieve her favorite diamonds, Wanda's smile crumbled.

Empty!

EXTENDED FAMILY

After his parents died, Zeke went to live with his uncle Ted, the writer.

An expert on holidays, he'd recently published a book on the history of Halloween.

Despite his newfound loneliness, Zeke felt at home relatively quickly.

Some mornings, they cooked omelets, potatoes, and toast, washing it all down with orange juice or black coffee.

Some nights, they talked about love and loss and fear and fishing. And sometimes they even talked about what made Neil Young so good and Neil Diamond so bad.

THE FUNERAL PARTY

He'd never baked bread before, wasn't confident of his recipe. Dusted with rogue flour, he pulled the loaf from the oven. It crackled, singing as it met cool air.

With serrated knife he sliced and buttered thin pieces, handing one to each relative around the room.

Best not tell them of the finely ground addition of Grandpa's metatarsal to the flour.

A cousin from Albuquerque remarked, "Remember that song Grandpa always sang? What was it?"

With his mouth half-full, a previously shy and tone-deaf relative from Amarillo effortlessly lilted through the catchy tune.

Then, to a stunned crowd: "Good bread."

AT REST

One day the apparition realized the house he'd been haunting had long since been deserted.

He ceased rattling and knocking, unscrewed his face, floated gently to the ground.

"Home," he intoned. Then, again: "Hoooooome."

He smiled at the sound of his own lonesome voice in the halls.

ACKNOWLEDGMENTS

Without the love, support, and guidance provided by certain people, this collection might never have come to fruition. Heartfelt thanks are due to Christian Kiefer for his friendship, feedback, and belief in these tiny tales; Lois Ann Abraham, for her wise and creative editorial touch; Don Reid, for his typesetting prowess; Lottie Aston, my wonderful wife, for putting up with me while I wrote every day; and to all the folks who followed the original *Flash Fiction 365* blog, for their time and dedication.

In 2009, I wrote and posted one extremely short story every day, the length of each determined by the rolling of two eight-sided dice, each tale falling between 11 and 88 words. During the month of December, while finishing the original experiment, I decided to invite readers of the blog to submit story titles and then composed micro-stories based on those suggestions. I am indebted to the following people for providing the following titles: "Hot Peppers" (5) by Nichola Owens, "In Flew the *Elegance*" (27) by Dylan Oliver, "Goose Attack!" (42) by Christian Kiefer, "Sassy Pants" (45) by Mary Bond, "Whirling Dervishes" (52) by Jeffrey

Callison, "Land, Grant!"(63) by Bradly Nabors, "Falling Stars" (75) by Kelley Darrah-Kordonowy, "Bucky Called Dibs" (76) by Raj Hundal, "Gridlock" (79) by Al Jacobus, "Where'd the Cheese Go?" (83) by Lottie Aston, "1989" (93) by Donna Morello, and "Gam Chammleman Takes Back His Time" (94) by Michael Rahhal. Thanks to all thirty-one people who submitted titles. And thanks in advance to all who upload readings to YouTube.

ABOUT THE AUTHOR

Jason Sinclair Long studied Theater and American Literature at UC Santa Cruz and earned his MFA in Playwriting from UCLA. He is a former member of Blue Man Group and currently teaches, writes, drums, gardens, and plays board games in Northern California with his wife and two sons.

AN INVITATION

To add your voice to a living experiment, pick a favorite story, video yourself reading it in an interesting location, and upload it to YouTube with **#TinyGiants** and **#AdLumen** in the description.

Use the URL below or scan this QR-Code to see the readings.

http://bit.ly/tinygiants